SOME STUFF YOU MIGHT NEED TO KNOW

OK, before we get started, let's talk about me. After all, I'm the one telling the story.

My name is Mark Taylor and I'm an Astral Guardian. So are my dad, mum and sister. We've been sent to Earth to protect the world from super villains, aliens and all sorts of nasty stuff. We're part of an intergalactic police force whose job it is to make sure the universe stays safe. Astral Command (who are in charge of just about everything) give us our orders but, if things go wrong, they send the Astral Knights to sort things out.

You don't want to mess with the Astral Knights. They can blow up planets! Here on Earth we're known as superheroes. Dad is Captain Valiant. He can fly and has super-strength. He also likes bacon sandwiches and eats lots of them, but that's not really a superpower.

Mum is
Ms Victory. She is
super-clever,
super-fast and tells
Dad off for eating
lots of bacon
sandwiches. She does
all the scientific and
technical stuff.

My sister, Emma,
is Moon Girl.
She can move
objects with her
mind and has a cloak of
invisibility. She is also
very moody and
likes to thump me.

I'm Dynamic Boy. Yes, I know it's a stupid name. But if you think that's stupid, you should see my costume. Dad and Mum look great in red, white and blue. Emma is in black and silver, but looks even better when she's invisible. My costume is black and gold with a lightning  flash down the front. I look like an electric bee. Even my powers aren't much good. All I can do is fly and create illusions. Who cares about that?

When they're not being superheroes, Dad and Mum are Robert and Louise Taylor, IT consultants. When we're not being superheroes, Emma and I are just two normal children . . .. apart from the superpowers, of course. But we're only allowed to use our powers when we're fighting super villains, aliens and all that other nasty stuff. When we're out with our friends we can't use them. When we're at home or school, Mum and Dad want us to be like everyone else. Superpowers are banned, even though Emma and I sometimes use them when we think Mum and Dad won't find out!

We live in a normal house . . . well, almost normal. We have a laboratory hidden under the washing machine in the utility room. That's where we watch out for all those super villains and aliens. I suppose you could call it our secret base, although it's not very big. It's full of computers and strange machines that I don't understand. It's also the place where we go to contact Astral Command – but we only do that in emergencies. We're meant to be able to do this job on our own.

The only thing in the lab that really impresses

me is the particle web. It can transport us all over the world in an instant, which is very impressive for something that looks like a giant, green, glowing bogey. At least, *I* think it does. Mum's the

only one who really knows how the particle web works and she doesn't like me calling it a giant, green, glowing bogey. She says it's too important to make fun of. Well, she *is* super-clever, so I suppose she knows what she's talking about.

And that's it really. Apart from fighting monsters, super villains and protecting the world from alien attacks, we're just a normal family. Of course, we probably have a few more adventures than most normal families and I imagine, if you've read this far, that you're ready for another one.

Well, here it is . . .

CHAPTER 1

'Are we there yet?' Dad asked.

I hoped he wasn't trying to be funny. This wasn't the right time for jokes. Dad didn't sound like he was trying to be funny. Maybe he honestly believed we were nearly there . . . except that he frowned, shook his head and drummed his fingers on the steering wheel.

'It would be nice if we didn't have much further to go,' he said. 'It's getting very dark and I can't see the road clearly.'

'It's the middle of the night and it's raining,'
Emma muttered. 'Of course you can't see the
road clearly.'

It wasn't the middle of the night. It was only
ten o'clock – although sitting on the back seat of
an over-warm car, with no mobile-phone signal
and a tablet computer which needed recharging,
it might as well have been the middle of the
night. We'd been travelling for eight hours and I
was sooo tired. I'd tried sleeping, but it wasn't
easy with my head wedged between a seatbelt
and a car door. It also wasn't easy when Emma
was in one of her I-told-you-so moods.

She folded her arms and
mumbled something under
her breath. Ever since Dad
had made Mum get out
the road atlas –
which was just
after he'd had
an argument
with the

satnav and punched it – Emma had done a lot of mumbling under her breath.

Thankfully, Mum and Dad didn't have super-hearing.

Emma grunted, squirmed under her seatbelt and spread across the back seat. I'd managed to build a barrier between us out of a cool-box and a travel rug, but I was sure Emma had used the power to move objects with her mind to slide the cool-box closer to me.

Not that this was a problem. One of the reasons I'd built the barrier was because I didn't like to sit too close to Emma. On long car journeys she often got travelsick. It's not much fun sitting in a puddle of vomit in an over-warm car. The more Emma pushed me away from her, the further I got from being covered in her lunch!

'The rain's getting worse,' Dad said. 'It really would be a good idea if we got there soon.'

A gust of wind whistled around us. Rain hammered on the roof. I was sure I heard thunder, although, looking at Mum in the passenger seat, gripping the road atlas so hard the pages had twisted, it was easy to imagine it wasn't a rumble of thunder but a low, angry growl.

'Robert,' she said through clenched teeth, 'we would be there by now if you'd listened to me. I'm sure all of us would prefer to be tucked up in soft, warm beds in the luxury suite I've booked at the Glenmore Hotel. However, because you were so sure that it would be quicker if we left the

motorway at Junction Twelve rather than Junction Eleven, and because you were convinced that this road would be a shortcut back to the dual carriageway, I have no idea where we are!'

Emma pushed her knees into the back of Mum's seat.

'This is so embarrassing,' she said. 'We're superheroes. We travel around the world fighting super villains and we can't even find a hotel in Scotland.'

'Emma, will you please be quiet,' Mum replied.

'If you've nothing useful to say then don't say anything at all.' She turned round. 'And I've told you before, sit up and give Mark some room.'

Emma had no intention of giving me some room. She deliberately spread out so that she was almost lying flat.

'I told you this would happen,' she said. 'I told you it wasn't a good idea to have a normal holiday like normal people. When normal people go on holidays they normally get lost!'

Mum took a deep breath. She was trying to control her temper. This weekend away had been her idea. She said it was too easy to think of ourselves as only superheroes and that we ought to spend more time just being a family – which was why we were on our way to the Glenmore Hotel where we were to enjoy two days of family stuff. Mum hadn't explained what this family stuff was, but she told us we'd definitely enjoy it.

'Emma,' Mum said, 'I'm getting a little tired of having

to explain this. For the last time, the reason why we do things like normal people – and that includes getting lost – is to remind us that we can't rely on our superpowers to solve all our problems. We have to rely on each other as well. Sometimes superpowers take second place to trust, respect and . . .'

'You don't need superpowers to read a map,' Emma muttered.

'I can read the map!' Mum shouted. 'It's just that your father can't follow instructions!'

It seemed to me that sometimes being normal was more difficult than being superheroes. I rested my face against the window and stared into the dark. The beam of the car's headlights reflected off the rain. The road we followed was a thin strip of tarmac bordered by grass, mud and stone. I couldn't remember how long it had been since I'd seen a house or anything that looked like a building. Before it got really dark, there had been a few sheep and lots of craggy hills but even they'd vanished now.

I looked at my mobile phone. There was still no signal. I guessed Mum would have felt better if she'd been able to let the hotel know we were on our way, but Dad had been so sure he knew where he was going and Mum had been so sure she could find out where we were on the map, that by the time we realised they couldn't do either of these things our phones didn't work. And what was even worse, it had been at least two hours since we'd stopped for a break.

'I need the toilet,' I said.

Emma sniffed and kicked me.

'He's right,' she said. 'Farty Boy's dropped one.'

'No, I haven't. Besides, that's not why I need to go.'

'Well, someone does.'

I sniffed. Emma was right.

'It's probably Dad,' I said.

'It wasn't me,' Dad replied.

'It was last time,' I said.

'No, I explained that. It's this seat. If you sit in the right spot it makes a funny noise.'

Dad tried to find the right spot but there was no noise.

'Robert,' Mum said, pointing at the dashboard, 'I hate to interrupt this oh-so-important conversation, but could you tell me what that red light means . . . You know, the one near the fuel gauge?'

'What light?' Dad swallowed hard. 'Oh, that light. Well, I suppose that means I should have stopped for petrol before we left the motorway, just like you said.'

'Yes, it does, doesn't it?' Mum let out a strange, gurgling scream. The road atlas hit the dashboard. 'Why do you never listen to a word I say? I can't believe you can be so ... so ...'

We never got a chance to find out what Dad could be so because, at that moment, he jerked the steering wheel to the right. I slammed into the car door. Emma slid across the seat and thudded into the cool-box, which thudded into me. Tyres screeched over tarmac and there was a sharp crack under us. When we stopped, we found ourselves facing across the road rather than along it, tilted back with our headlights pointing up into the sky.

Screech!!

Rain rattled against the windows. Mum and Dad looked round to make sure Emma and I were all right. Apart from being tangled in our seatbelts, we were fine. Emma unknotted herself, jabbing me in the ribs with her elbows. She was about to unclip her belt when she straightened and pointed through the windscreen.

'I don't want to worry anyone,' she said, 'but should something like that be on a road like this on a stormy night in Scotland?'

Mum, Dad and I looked where Emma pointed. Standing in front of the car, caught in the glare of the headlights, battered by the wind and drenched with rain, was one of the strangest creatures I had ever seen.

Now, I've seen quite a few strange creatures in my time — some of them real and some of them illusions which I've made up while fighting super villains — but this one was so weird it would have taken a better imagination than mine to invent it.

The creature stood upright. It had the body of a man and the head and wings of an insect. Its grey skin was so thin I could see the veins and muscle underneath. The creature's arms and legs looked like they'd been stretched as far as they would go before snapping. A pair of fly-like eyes stared at me from a head that jerked and twitched. Long antennae wriggled as its wings beat against the wind. The creature wore no clothes, but around its waist was a black belt with

a large, metal canister hanging from it.

'So that's what ran across the road,' Dad said. 'I thought it was a sheep.'

I wished it had been a sheep. I wouldn't have minded fighting a bad-tempered sheep. This thing looked a bit more dangerous. A pair of drooling mandibles opened. Spindly arms stretched out. Barbed talons flexed on three-fingered hands. Clawed feet splashed through muddy puddles.

Yes, I suppose if it had been a sheep, we would probably have stood a chance. As it was, we were too easy a target sitting inside the car. Perhaps if we'd acted quicker, we could have put up a better fight. But there was more than one strange creature to deal with – there were two.

The other one ripped the roof off. Then it pulled the car doors away. As metal clanged and glass shattered, I blinked through the wind and rain to see flashes of arms, legs, claws and . . . feathers. Black feathers beat against our heads as something screeched and squawked above us.

Mum shouted something. I don't know what

she said. I was too busy trying to unclip my seatbelt with wet fingers. There was a

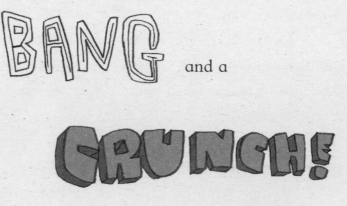 and a

The insect creature landed on the bonnet. I saw Dad throw a punch as it dived at him. There was a hiss, like escaping steam, then Dad slumped across the steering wheel and his head hit the horn.

The blare sounded like a scream.

A shadow fell across Mum. Her arms went over her head as something wrapped itself round her. The hiss got louder and then she also collapsed, her limp body thudding against the dashboard. I looked around for Emma, thinking that maybe she could do something with her powers. Only she'd gone. There were just the

shredded ends of her seatbelt left, and when I looked back at Mum and Dad, they had gone as well.

So that was it – I was on my own against these things. I fought to get free, only it was too late. I heard the hissing. I smelt a strange, sweet odour, which was so powerful I almost choked. I felt dizzy. My arms and legs seemed to float away from my body. My head seemed to float away from my neck.

Not that I minded any more. My fear and anger had evaporated in the sweet smell. I didn't care about anything – not the wind or the rain or the creatures. Even Mum, Dad and Emma didn't seem to matter. After all, I couldn't help them. All I could do was float away in that sweet smell as it made me feel . . .

CHAPTER 2

. . . sick.

I suppose I must have fallen asleep. When I woke, I was lying in a room, on a bed, fully clothed, with my head feeling as if there was a brick where my brain should have been. I tried to sit up, only the brick wouldn't let me. My neck and shoulders ached and, when I moved, the ache spread down my arms and legs. My stomach felt as if there was something swimming around inside it, waiting to leap up my throat and dive out of my mouth. I decided it was a good idea not to move.

I had no idea where I was. There was nothing in the room I recognised. I could still remember the creatures and the car and, for a moment, I wondered if it had all been a bad dream. Maybe I was at the Glenmore Hotel. Maybe I'd fallen asleep on the back seat and had a nightmare. But if that was the case, why was I lying on a bed fully clothed? That didn't make any sense. And why were my clothes damp?

I turned my head to look around the room. Emma lay on a bed opposite me. She was also fully clothed. There were wet patches on her sweatshirt and trousers. No, it couldn't have been a dream. Something had attacked us in the car and brought us here. And if so, where was here and, more importantly, where were Mum and Dad?

Daylight came through narrow windows set high in the walls near the ceiling. Outside, I saw a grim, grey sky. The room was large and clean with brown carpets and cream walls. There was a wardrobe, a chest of drawers and two armchairs. Oil paintings of birds hung in ornate, wooden frames above the beds. Through a door near Emma's bed, I saw a sink, a toilet and a bath with a shower curtain.

On the far side of the room, next to a table laid with cups and plates, was a large wooden door with a very big lock. A man stood by the door. He wore a green, chunky jumper and faded jeans. His black hair was a greasy mess and his straggly beard was matted. As he met my gaze, he walked towards me but stopped before he got too close. The man looked nervous, as if unsure whether he should be in the room.

'I've prepared breakfast for you,' he said, pointing at the table. His voice was soft and low. 'It's not much, I'm afraid, but it's nutritious and will help you get over the effects of the gas. You do like porridge, don't you? I've eaten porridge ever since I was a boy. My mother said it was good for me.' The man reached into his trouser pocket and took out a bunch of keys. He played with them as he spoke. 'And you should always trust your mother, shouldn't you? I mean, a boy's best friend is his mother.' He looked at the keys one by one, as if counting them: 'I imagine you must have lots of questions. I know I would

have lots of questions.' He paused, as if waiting for me to speak. 'No? Well, it doesn't matter. You'll feel better when you've had some porridge.'

The brick in my head was getting lighter. I managed to pull myself up and pay more attention to the man. He attempted a smile, only his beard got in the way of his lips. If he'd had a shave and a wash, and if his clothes hadn't been covered in stains, I imagine he would have looked quite respectable.

As it was, he was the kind of man who made you itch just to look at him. I guessed he was in his forties. His greasy, black hair was tinged with grey at the sides.

'I'm Dr Alistair MacDeth,' the man said. 'This,' he indicated the room, 'is my home.' He looked at the keys again. 'It's actually a castle. It's been in my family for generations. There are lots of rooms. That's why I have all these keys. The doors have to be locked. Yes, that's very important. The doors have to be locked.'

So, he was some kind of doctor – probably a scientist. I suppose he could have been a Doctor of Philosophy, but I doubted it. In my experience, superheroes like us usually had to deal with death-rays and monsters rather than logical arguments – and the fact that Dr MacDeth wasn't surprised to find two children asleep in his castle proved that he knew a lot more than he was telling me. Whoever he was, he couldn't be trusted.

I heard a snuffle and a grunt. It was a snuffle and a grunt I'd heard many times before, usually in the morning, and usually when Emma pushed me out of the way to get to the bathroom. My sister wasn't at her best in the mornings and couldn't manage words until she'd been to the bathroom.

Emma dragged herself into a sitting position. She blinked and gazed round the room. She saw me, grunted again, burped and put her hand over her mouth.

'If you're going to be sick,' MacDeth said, 'I'd appreciate it if you'd use the bathroom. I don't have a cleaner any more, so if you make a mess, you'll have to clean it up yourself.'

Emma didn't need to be told twice. She ran for the bathroom and slammed the door behind her.

MacDeth sighed. 'I'm afraid the anaesthetic gas can make you a bit queasy,' he said. 'I designed it myself. It's basically a mix of nitrous oxide and . . .' He glanced at me and scowled. I had the feeling I'd done something to annoy him. 'She's not ill, is she? This sickness, it is just the gas, isn't it? There's nothing else I need to know about? And the other two, there's nothing wrong with them, is there? I can only make things right if there's nothing wrong with them.'

The bathroom door opened. Emma returned and dropped on to the bed. She rubbed her stomach and looked round the room again. She frowned at everything she saw, including Dr MacDeth.

'Are you room service?' she asked.

'No, I'm . . .' MacDeth seemed confused. He pointed at the table again. 'A little breakfast will help settle your stomach. It's only porridge but it's very nutritious. My mother always said —'

'I don't like porridge,' Emma interrupted.

MacDeth stared at the bowls on the table. His mouth opened but no sound came out.

'My mother . . .' he said again, ' . . . she always gave me porridge for breakfast. It's very nutritious.'

'I'm sure it is,' Emma replied. 'But I don't suppose your mother could do me some fresh orange juice and a couple of slices of toast.'

'My mother? No, I'm afraid she's . . .' MacDeth tensed. His head twitched and his teeth clenched. He made a strange whining sound. 'My mother is . . .' MacDeth started to tremble. The whine turned into a whimper. 'My mother is . . .'

MacDeth spun away and threw himself at the door. He fell to his knees, got up, lost his balance and crashed into the table. Bowls and

cups shattered. Porridge splashed over him and splattered across the walls. Clambering to his feet, MacDeth fumbled at the door handle and then lurched outside. When he grabbed the door to close it, he glared back at us.

'I am Dr Alistair MacDeth!' he shrieked. 'And my mother is dead! She's dead!'

The door slammed and the key scraped in the lock. There was a thud and a bang and then silence.

Emma tutted and shook her head. 'I only asked for orange juice and toast,' she said. 'I hate to think what would have happened if I'd asked for a bacon sandwich as well.'

CHAPTER 3

I groaned and swung my legs off the bed. I'd coped with the porridge, the orange juice and the toast but, at the mention of bacon sandwiches, the thing that was swimming around in my stomach decided to make one last attempt to escape.

It failed. Clenched teeth and a few deep breaths managed to keep it at bay. I had more important things to do than throw up. MacDeth had mentioned something about there being nothing wrong with the other two. I wasn't sure what he meant by nothing wrong — unless he was talking about an illness or something — but I guessed the other two were Mum and Dad; which meant they were probably somewhere in this castle, locked up like us.

A dollop of porridge slipped off the wall and splattered on the floor.

'We have to get out of here,' I said to Emma.

She gave me the kind of look she usually gave Dad when he told her to tidy her room. 'And who put you in charge?' she asked. 'Since I'm the oldest, I'll decide what we're going to do. I think we should stay where we are. I feel terrible and you don't look much better.'

'Stay where we are? Are you joking?' I went to the door and tried the handle. I shouldn't have bothered. The door wasn't going to open. 'You remember being attacked by those creatures, don't you?'

Emma shrugged. 'Maybe,' she said. 'I was hoping it might have been one of your illusions.'

'Why would I have created an illusion like that?'

'I don't know. Perhaps you were bored.'

'Well, I didn't create any illusions. This is all very real. And as for Dr Alistair

MacDeth, I don't think he's the local GP making a house call. He expected us to be here. After all, he made us breakfast. I bet he knows a lot more about what's going on than we do.'

Emma belched again and rubbed her stomach. 'Yes, all right, Sherlock,' she said, 'I get it. What you're saying is that you think we're being held prisoner by a mad scientist.'

'I think it would be a good idea to assume we are,' I replied, 'which is why I think it would also be a good idea to find Mum and Dad.'

Emma looked round the room as if she'd only just realised we were on our own.

'But if Mum and Dad aren't here . . .' she began.

'Exactly,' I said. 'If Mum and Dad aren't here, then we have to ask ourselves why they aren't here. Let's be honest, if they were awake like us, it would be a lot noisier. Dad would be breaking down walls and smashing doors by now. No, something's wrong. We can't wait for Mum and Dad to come looking for us, we have to get out of this room, get hold of Dr MacDeth and find out what he's done with them.'

I tried to open the door again. I don't know

why, because it was just as secure as it was last time. Then I remembered the windows and

looked up. They appeared easy enough to break but they were too small and narrow. I certainly wouldn't be able to squeeze through them and as for Emma, she was taller and broader than me. Without Dad's super-strength, we wouldn't be able to make a big enough hole. There seemed to be no way out. Feeling completely useless, I kicked an overturned bowl of porridge into the wall.

Emma stared at the broken pieces. 'You're not telling me everything, are you?' she said. 'What's up, Mark? You're not usually this stressed, even when we're doing all the dangerous superhero stuff.'

Staring at the porridge as it soaked into the carpet, I wondered whether to tell Emma what

MacDeth had said while she was being sick in the bathroom. After all, I didn't know for definite who the other two were. All I had were suspicions. But I didn't really have a choice. Emma had a right to know. In the car, Mum had said we had to show respect for each other. This wasn't about being superheroes. This was about being a family.

I'd only just got to the part about MacDeth saying he could make things right, when an invisible force grabbed me and shoved me away from the door. It was Emma. She'd used her power to move objects with her mind to push me aside before lifting my bed off the floor, hurling the mattress, pillows and duvet into a corner and turning the frame on its side.

'All right,' she said, 'I'm convinced. We need to get out of here and find Mum and Dad.'

The bed shot across the room and hammered into the door. The frame banged against the wood again and again. There was a lot of crunching and snapping but the door remained intact. It was the bed that broke apart. It whistled past me again and again. I had to shield my eyes as the frame exploded. Soon, there was nothing left of the bed except broken wood.

Emma got up to have a look at what she'd done. The door was scratched and dented but still firmly locked. She glanced up at the windows. I knew what she was thinking.

'They're too small,' I said. 'We won't be able to get through them.'

'I know,' Emma replied, 'but if you flew up and had a look outside, there might be something I could pull through the window . . . you know, a piece of metal or stone . . .'

It wasn't a good idea. Whatever we pulled through the window wasn't going to be big enough or strong enough to break down the door or smash the bricks around the windows, and Emma knew it. Probably feeling as useless as me, she kicked a piece of wood so hard that it flew across the room and hit the wardrobe.

The wardrobe doors creaked open. Inside there were four fur coats, which looked very old and threadbare. As the doors swung loose on their hinges, wood scraped against wood and a solid darkness seemed to ooze from between the coats. It may have only been shadow, but it was as if there was something inside the wardrobe crawling into the room.

'Please, don't hurt me,' a wheezy, high-pitched voice said. 'Alistair told me to come up here. I was only watching you through the spyhole in the wardrobe to make sure you were all right.'

Emma squealed and put her hand to her mouth. It looked like she was going to be sick again.

'I'm sorry if I startled you, but I've never met a superhero before. You are a superhero, aren't you? I saw you move the bed. Did you do it with your mind? I don't know anyone who can move objects with their mind except a superhero. I suppose you could be a witch. But you don't have a wand, and Alistair says there's no such thing as magic. But there are superheroes. Yes, even Alistair knows superheroes are real.'

Limping out of the wardrobe, nosing its way through the fur coats, was a fat, pink, hairless rat . . . At least, I think it was a rat. It was far too big for a normal rat – about the same size as a cat – and, as well as not having any fur, the head was too big: it had a typical rodent's pointed snout but there was a large, bulbous growth at the back, like a football. The head rolled from side to side and seemed to be about to fall off and bounce across the floor.

The rat stepped down from the wardrobe and stared at us with white eyes.

'I suppose I should introduce myself properly,' it said. 'Mummy always taught me to be polite. My name is Helen MacDeth. You've already met my brother, Alistair. I hope he made you welcome.'

CHAPTER 4

Okay, so the rat could talk. Given everything else that had happened, I shouldn't have been surprised. First we were attacked by two strange creatures on a stormy night, then we'd woken up in a castle, and now we were listening to an oversized, deformed rodent who claimed to be the sister of a mad scientist called Dr MacDeth – the pieces of this puzzle were fitting together in a way I really didn't like.

The rat limped closer. She stretched out a

scrawny paw as if she wanted to shake hands.

'You are a superhero, aren't you?' she said again. 'Please say that you are. You must be. I saw what you did. You have to be a superhero, because if you're not, I don't know what we'll do. Superheroes are meant to help people and we need help.'

The rat put her paws over her face and started to cry. Her sobs came in short, shrill squeaks. The sound was so pitiful I wanted to feel sorry for her, only it was hard to feel sorry for a giant pink, hairless rat. I didn't even like rats when they were small, brown and furry. 'Do you want me to

get rid of it?' Emma whispered. 'You know, smash it with a piece of wood or throw it back in the wardrobe?'

'No, please!' The rat looked up. 'I don't want to hurt you. It's not my fault I'm like this. It was Alistair. He said he could . . . he said he would be able to . . .' The rat rocked backwards and forwards. 'We all believed him. We all trusted him . . . and I know he didn't want this to happen . . . But he says he can fix it. Now that you're here he says he can . . . but what if he can't? What if . . .' The rat put her paws over her face again.

You know, it would have been bad enough having to deal with a talking rat. But having to deal with a depressed talking rat was something Emma and I definitely didn't have time to do. We had to find Mum and Dad.

'Do you know where your brother is?' I snapped. 'Can you take us to him?'

The rat backed away, trembling and twitching. 'He's probably in the laboratory,' she said. 'That's where he does all his work and that's where the other two . . . but you mustn't hurt Alistair. He's too important. He's the only one who knows what went wrong and the only one who can change us back. And he's not a bad man. It was Mother. She was sick. She was dying. Alistair only wanted to save Mother. He's so clever. He knows so much about cells and biology. He said that . . .'

The rat looked at the wardrobe. She stared into the darkness behind the fur coats.

'A superhero,' she said. 'You're a superhero. I watched you. If Alistair knew you were a superhero he might be able to get you to help him. You have powers. Maybe those powers would make it easier to find a cure.'

With a burst of speed I didn't think possible, the rat darted for the wardrobe and leapt inside. The last I saw of the rodent was her grotesque head rolling from side to side as she scrambled between the fur coats and vanished into the darkness.

'Much as I hate to admit it,' Emma said, 'the

talking rat kind of proves your mad-scientist theory. Now I suppose you're going to say something really stupid like "Let's follow that thing".'

I went to the wardrobe. Pushing aside the coats, I saw that the panel at the back was open and led into a narrow, unlit brick tunnel. The

echo of the rat's claws on the stone floor taunted me through the gloom. I glanced round at Emma. She shook her head.

'No, don't tell me,' she said. 'I bet there's a secret passage in the wardrobe. There has to be. After all, what else would you find inside a wardrobe in a mad scientist's castle?'

'Not only are you right about the secret passage,' I replied, 'but you're also right about what I'm going to say. I think we should follow the talking rat.'

CHAPTER 5

Although we didn't really follow the rat.

The echo of the rodent's claws soon faded and the light from the room quickly dimmed after only a few steps along the passage. Now there was nothing to follow except the walls and floor, and they only went one way – down. We had to rely on our hands and feet to guide us. All our other senses were useless. There was no sound other than our footsteps and no smell other than the musty odour of damp brick.

It was at times like this that I wished I had a really useful superpower, like being able to see in the dark. When you're walking into a blackness so thick you can almost feel it, it would be nice to know if there's something waiting to leap out and get you.

Emma grabbed my shoulder. I was so startled I almost swore at her.

'You do realise this could be a trap?' she said. 'For all we know, the rat could have lied. Maybe it wants us to follow it down here. Maybe it plans to . . . well, I don't know what it plans to do. But I don't think we should trust a talking rat.'

'I don't trust it,' I replied. 'We're following the rat because we have to find Mum and Dad and this is the only way out of the room.'

I stopped and sniffed. There was now a different smell mixed in with the damp brick. It was bleach or antiseptic. Emma sniffed as well.

'It smells like a hospital,' she said.

'Or a laboratory,' I replied.

Both of us quickened our pace. It wasn't long before I felt the slope level out and the passage widen. Emma and I held on to each other. If this was a trap, then we were well and truly caught. If only we could see!

My mind created all sorts of monsters out of the darkness. I saw fangs and horns, heard growls and hissing, felt claws tearing at my clothes. Something thudded, something slithered

and something crunched. And then my fingers found the one thing that had the power to defeat all the terrors my imagination had created – a light switch!

I turned it on. Above our heads, a line of strip lights flickered into life. Blinking in the glare, Emma and I found ourselves at the end of a long, straight corridor. The left side was solid brick. The right side had a line of six grey, metal doors. Each one had a bar across the middle, which slid into the wall like a bolt.

Opposite us, at the end of the corridor, was a seventh door – or rather, there was a sheet of metal that looked like a door. It had no hinges, handle or bolt, but it was the same size and shape as the other doors – grey, plain and clearly designed to keep something in or out.

'Okay,' Emma said, 'so we've left a locked room and ended up in a dungeon. This plan is working really well.'

'I don't think this is a dungeon,' I replied. 'I think it's something worse. Look over there.'

At the end of the corridor, near the sheet of metal set into the wall, was a mop and a bucket. A dripping tap stuck out of the wall over the bucket and, piled up beside the tap,

were large, blue tins of disinfectant. I shivered as
I wondered why so much disinfectant might be
needed . . .?

'At least that explains the smell,' Emma said.
She went to the nearest door and examined the
bolt and hinges. 'There's no dirt or rust and the
bolt looks new. Someone's definitely been down
here recently.'

'Yes, but why have they been down here?'

Emma looked along the corridor. 'Where do
you think that rat's gone?' she said. 'It must have
come this way. Maybe it went through one of
these.'

Emma's hand reached for the bolt. I got to her before she slid it back.

'The rat is too small to open these doors,' I said. 'If it's down here, then it must have gone that way.' I nodded towards the sheet of metal at the end of the corridor.

'But that's a dead end,' Emma said.

I wasn't convinced. I walked up to the sheet of metal and examined it closely. It was also clean and rust free. There wasn't a scratch or dent in the surface and nothing that showed that the metal moved in any way. I pushed against it.

'I'm right, aren't I?' Emma said. 'It's a dead end.'

I went back to join her. 'Yes,' I said. 'It's a dead end.'

'So whether we like it or not . . .' Emma turned to the door again, ' . . . we either go through one of these doors or go back to the room.' She knocked and waited for a reply. 'You never know, just because the rat couldn't open a door doesn't mean that someone didn't open one for it.'

Emma knocked again. The rap of her knuckles echoed along the corridor. My sister had a habit of being annoyingly right. Yes, we did have to go through one of these doors or go back to our room. But I didn't want to do either. I thought about the deformed rat and the creatures that had attacked us. Sometimes, I didn't need my imagination to invent horrors. There were enough in my memories, locked behind doors that I didn't have to open.

Emma took hold of the bolt again. I stood back and nodded. As long as the lights stayed on, and as long as we had enough room, and as long as we acted quickly, Emma and I could take care

of ourselves . . . I hoped. It all depended what was behind the door.

Emma pushed the bolt. It slid far too easily and far too smoothly. I wanted to tell her to push it back, only my fear was overpowered by my curiosity. As soon as the bolt moved, I heard crying — a soft, gentle weeping. What was even more curious was that it sounded like a man who was crying.

The bolt slid all the way across and thudded to a stop. The door opened slowly. A thin, white hand with overlong fingers grasped the edge as a second hand grabbed the doorframe. The wrists attached to the hands were twisted and knobbly, as if the bones had been broken and put back in the wrong position. The arms attached to the wrists were bare and covered in cuts and scratches.

'Is that you, Alistair?' the crying man asked. 'Is it time to go to work again? I'm so tired. Couldn't I sleep for just a few more hours? The change . . . it's getting worse. Perhaps if I had more time to rest . . . Please? Could I just sleep for a few more hours?'

The crying turned into sobs. By now, Emma had backed away from the door. Her eyes were fixed on the hands and arms.

'Alistair?' the man said again. 'Is that you? Why don't you answer me?'

The door opened further and the man stumbled into the corridor, falling against the wall and sliding to his knees. He was horribly thin and wore nothing but a pair of striped pyjama bottoms. I was about to help him up when he raised his head. Where the man's eyes should have been there was now only skin. I froze at the sight.

'Alistair?' The man's head jerked from side to side. 'Alistair?'

'Emma,' I whispered, 'I think it would be a good idea if you —'

Only it was too late to do anything. The man shrieked and leapt at us, clawing blindly at the air until his long, bony fingers found something to grip – Emma.

CHAPTER 6

I suppose it was a mixture of fear and shock that made me and Emma slow to react. After all, using her thoughts, Emma could have picked up the man and thrown him back behind the door. Only she didn't. Instead, she scrambled away as the man tore at her clothes. Then she slipped and fell, banging her head on the bricks. When she landed, I could tell she was dazed and confused. She didn't fight back as the man pulled her towards him, dragging her across the floor with sharp, vicious tugs.

'You're not Alistair,' he said. 'Who are you? What do you want?' The eyeless head bent down and sniffed. 'What are you?' The man licked his lips. His tongue was much longer than a normal tongue. It tasted Emma's face. 'Are you to eat? Has Alistair sent food? I haven't eaten fresh meat for so long. Is that what you are — fresh meat?'

I couldn't wait for Emma to defend herself. I had to do something. Flying along the corridor, I hurled myself into the man. He howled, lost his grip and crashed into the wall. I managed to grab Emma and pull her with me. The man ended up in a thrashing, squealing heap. Emma and I ended up further along the corridor, closer to the sheet of metal and the tins of disinfectant.

I watched the man scrabble about on his hands and knees. His fingers scratched the bricks. His tongue slithered in and out.

'Fresh meat,' he whined. 'I want fresh meat. It's been so long since I tasted fresh meat!'

Emma sat with her back against the sheet of metal. She rubbed her head. 'Okay,' she said, 'so maybe it wasn't such a good idea to open that door.'

The man started to growl. Still on his hands and knees, he crawled closer to us. He stuck his head out and tasted the air with his tongue.

By now, Emma had recovered enough to use her powers. A tin of disinfectant flew down the corridor. But her aim was off and the tin smashed against the wall, sending thick, blue liquid splattering over the man's neck and back. He reared up, shrieking in pain.

'No! Please! It burns! I didn't mean to . . . I was only hungry! Please, I only wanted something to eat!'

The man threw himself at the nearest door. He tried to push it open, only it was bolted. As disinfectant dribbled down his pyjama bottoms, the man slammed back the bolt. He fell across the threshold, trying to drag himself away from the blue liquid.

He didn't get far. As soon as the man was halfway through the door, he stopped. There was a strange gurgling, slurping noise. The man's body jerked and twisted. His legs thrashed wildly. Then, as the slurp turned into a crunch, his legs went limp. There was more crunching and slurping. A jet of red liquid spurted

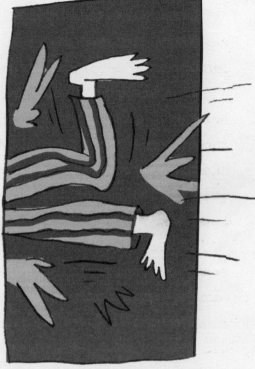

across the corridor and spattered over the floor.

The liquid looked like blood.

'Close that door,' I whispered to Emma.

'I'm trying to,' she whispered back. 'Only it won't move.'

I didn't want to think about why the door wouldn't move. Whatever was behind it — whatever had made those strange gurgling and slurping noises — was now free, and it was almost certainly going to come after us.

Emma and I were trapped. We had to find a way out. We couldn't risk opening another door so we had no choice. I faced the sheet of metal. It couldn't be a dead end. There had to be something on the other side, otherwise why would it be there? And that's when I saw it, in a darkened corner, high above us — a CCTV camera. We were being watched. Emma must have seen the camera as well. She was already on her feet, hammering at the metal with her fists.

We both banged and we both shouted. I even started to scream. To be honest, I didn't know what I was doing. My fists bounced off the metal as uselessly as my cries echoed off the walls. It wasn't long before my hands throbbed and my throat ached.

Emma and I fell silent at the same time. We were both out of breath. A faint, rasping wheeze whistled behind us. Emma looked at me.

'I hope you've suddenly become asthmatic,' she said, 'because if you haven't, I don't want to know what's making that noise.'

There was a thud. The wheeze got louder. There was a slap, then a scrape, another slap and another scrape. It sounded like something wet and heavy was being dragged across the floor.

I was about to hammer at the metal again when I felt a cold draft on my neck. There was a strange tickling sensation around my ankle. I wanted to reach down and scratch my foot, only the tickling turned into a warm dampness. Glancing at my feet, I saw the tip of a glistening, black tentacle slither over my shoe. 'I think we're in a lot of trouble,' I said.

The rasping wheeze turned into a crackling hiss. Emma and I grabbed each other's hands. We were both terrified and we both knew it. But if there was any chance of getting out of this alive, we had to turn round. We had to stop being frightened children and fight like the superheroes we were.

And I think we would have put up a pretty good fight if we'd had the chance – if the sheet of metal in front of us hadn't slid up into the roof and Dr MacDeth hadn't stood there.

The rat cowered at his feet. 'You see, Alistair?' she said. 'What did I tell you? He can fly and she can move objects with her mind. They have powers, Alistair, powers!'

I didn't care what we had. All I wanted was a way out. Emma and I barged past MacDeth. We stumbled up a short flight of steps and ran into a room that, even from the briefest glance, was obviously the laboratory.

I heard MacDeth shout, 'No, Mother, no. You must go back. It's not feeding time yet. And there's blood, Mother, blood. I've told you not to go near blood. It's not good for you.'

There were shrieks and snarls, groans and growls. The rat followed us up the steps and scuttled under a chair, wringing her paws as her deformed head rocked from side to side.

'Alistair believes me now,' she said. 'He watched you on the monitors. He saw your powers. He knows what you are. I told him you were superheroes. And now he believes me. He believes me!'

In the middle of the room, lying next to each other on a steel table, were Mum and Dad. They were both unconscious and held down by leather straps.

Emma and I rushed to the table. Our hands grabbed arms and slapped faces. Our fingers tore

at the leather straps. As we tried to wake Mum
and Dad, we glanced at the gruesome display of
scientific equipment around us. From what we
saw, it looked as if my suspicions about MacDeth
were correct. He was definitely a mad scientist
and he was definitely going to do some kind of
experiment on Mum and Dad.

There were trays of surgical instruments,

bottles of chemicals, microscopes, syringes, bandages and jars of green, murky liquid in which floated human organs, dissected animals and deformed creatures with multiple heads and severed limbs. Books and papers lay scattered over tables littered with test tubes, Bunsen burners, tripods and beakers. Next to a door on the far side of the room, was a sink. It was full of water, which had a brown, oily scum on the surface.

After struggling with the straps and buckles, they fell away. But Mum and Dad were still unconscious. They were going to be difficult to move, even with our powers. Knowing that we had to protect them, Emma and I turned to face

MacDeth as the metal sheet clanged shut and his footsteps sounded on the steps. When he appeared,

he was the same dishevelled
man he'd always been.
The only difference was that
there was blood on his hands
and, as he walked into the
lab, his shoes left red,
sticky footprints.

He ignored me and Emma and crossed to a
white wall cabinet. He opened it and took out a
bottle and a syringe. His fingers left bloody
smears on the cabinet's doors. He filled the
syringe from the bottle.

'I really am sorry about this,' he said. 'You have
to believe me. I didn't want this to happen.'

I didn't know what MacDeth planned to do
with the syringe and I didn't
want to find out.

'Emma,' I shouted, 'see if
you can move Mum and
Dad with your thoughts.
I'll take care of the
mad scientist!'

I was already in the air, ready to fly at MacDeth and snatch the syringe from him. Only I couldn't move. Something held me by the trousers. There was a hand on my waistband!

'It's all right, Mark,' Dad said, pulling me down, 'I'll deal with the mad scientist. If he comes near us with that syringe, I'll stick it somewhere very painful.'

CHAPTER 7

Fortunately for Dr MacDeth, Dad didn't have to stick the syringe anywhere. Sitting down at a table covered with small, glass bottles, MacDeth rolled up his sleeve and injected himself in the arm. He did it so quickly and calmly it was obvious he'd injected himself many times before.

'I really am sorry,' he said again, dropping the used syringe into a plastic bin. 'This isn't how it was meant to be.' He closed his eyes and tears rolled down his cheeks. He started mumbling to

himself. 'If only you'd been here at the beginning. The initial results were so promising. Mother seemed to improve and the four of us were like supermen. We didn't need to sleep. We were stronger, fitter . . . It was incredible. I'd never felt so . . . The weeks all rolled into one. Time became meaningless. We didn't even notice anything had gone wrong until . . .' He looked at his hands, staring at his fingers as if they didn't belong to him. 'If only you'd been here at the beginning. We were like supermen.'

By now, Mum and Dad were fully awake. They stretched, groaned and looked round the laboratory. I don't think any of us were really paying attention to MacDeth. Mum was too busy making sure we were all okay. The only thing that made her take notice of the mumbling scientist was a small needle-mark in her arm and a similar one in Dad's.

While Mum examined the marks, Emma and I explained what had happened to us – about waking up in the room, meeting the rat and fighting the creature in the corridor. We told her what little we knew about Dr MacDeth and what we suspected he'd been doing in his castle. Not surprisingly, Mum's expression darkened as we talked. By the time we'd finished, she strode over to

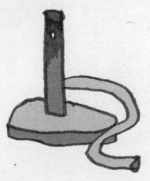

MacDeth and pointed to her arm.

'What did you inject us with?' she demanded.

'Just a sedative,' MacDeth replied. 'Nothing that would harm you in any way. I had to keep your bodies fresh. I didn't want any toxins in your bloodstream.'

Mum grabbed MacDeth by the collar. She almost pulled him out of his chair.

'You'd better be telling me the truth!' she yelled.

'I promise! It was only a sedative!' MacDeth cried. 'As soon as my sister told me about the girl, I thought you might be superheroes as well. The only other thing I injected was a stimulant to wake you up. You're too valuable to damage. You're the breakthrough I've been waiting for. You're my good luck!'

Mum pushed MacDeth away. 'Luck?' she said. 'This isn't luck, this is madness. What have you been doing here, MacDeth?' She looked round at the specimen jars and scientific equipment. A faint scratching made her glance at the steel table in the middle of the room. The rat had crept under it and now watched her. Mum took a sharp intake of breath. 'Of course – hybrid DNA. You've been creating hybrid DNA. That explains the creatures which attacked us and the talking rat. You've combined human and animal DNA and this is the result.'

'No!' MacDeth shouted. 'This isn't how it was meant to be. If you'd seen us at the beginning, you'd know. We were like supermen!'

Mum slapped MacDeth's face. 'You were never supermen. You were monsters!' she yelled. 'You've been experimenting with hybrid DNA and this is what's happened! That's why you kidnapped us. You needed uncontaminated tissue to repair the damage, didn't you? Our tissue, our organs, our clean DNA!' Mum slapped MacDeth again. 'You only wanted us for spare parts. If you hadn't found out we were superheroes, you'd have cut us all up and put us in jars just like the rest of your experiments!'

Mum slapped MacDeth a third time. Her hands became fists and she kept hitting him, beating him across the head and neck until Dad pulled her away.

MacDeth howled like a frightened child. He fell to his knees and threw up his arms. 'Yes,' he bawled, 'I did plan to use your organs and DNA. But I had no choice!' He pulled up his sleeve and showed Mum his arm. It was pitted with needle marks. 'I was so desperate I even experimented on myself and now I have to inject a viral suppressant every six hours to control the changes. First it was my mother, then my friends, then my sister and now me. I have three days at the most before I'm like them. That's why I had to find fresh

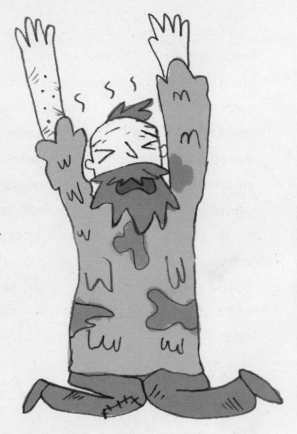

bodies. But now that you're here, I don't need your organs and DNA. I need your knowledge. You're superheroes. You've fought super villains and saved the world. With your skills and powers, you must be able to find a way to save us!'

Mum was in no mood to listen. Dad had to keep her from attacking MacDeth again. He lifted her across the room and spoke to her firmly and quietly. To be honest, I felt like hitting MacDeth as well. It wasn't just because he'd planned to use us in his experiments. I wanted to hit him because, like so many people, MacDeth thought that having superpowers was the same as being all-powerful. It wasn't. Some situations were so bad it was impossible to change them – and I had the horrible feeling this was going to be one of those situations.

MacDeth slumped to the floor and rolled up in a ball, crying like a baby. The rat came out from under the table and sat next to her brother. She stroked his head with her paw.

'Please, don't hurt him,' she said. 'I told you, he's not a bad man. He was only trying to help. It was Mummy, you see. He couldn't bear to see Mummy so ill.'

His mother? I remembered the thing in the corridor that Emma and I had been too scared to look at. I glanced down at my foot, where a black tentacle had slithered. I could still feel the warm dampness of its touch.

'He told us your mother was dead,' I said.

The rat rested her head on MacDeth's shoulder. 'No, not dead,' she said. 'But didn't you see what Mummy has become? Isn't that almost as bad as being dead? I blame Daddy. It's all his fault. He was a scientist, like Alistair. He worked for the government doing top-secret things. This was his laboratory. But he was very strict. He never allowed us down here and the door was always locked. When we were children, we crept down to listen to what was going on. It was horrible . . . all these frightening sounds and awful smells. But Alistair thought it was wonderful.

He so wanted to be
like Daddy. He so wanted
Mummy to admire him the
way she admired Daddy.'

    The rat looked up
at the specimen jars.
'Daddy died on the day Alistair got his first
research post at the university. After the funeral,
Alistair persuaded Mummy to let him use the
laboratory for his own experiments. It wasn't
long after that Mummy became ill. Alistair
couldn't bear to see her in so much pain. He did
everything he could to save her. I think his friends
only volunteered to help with his work because it
meant they could live in a castle and do what
they wanted. Clive, Alfred and
Lewis could be very silly. When they
weren't busy with experiments,
they drank a lot and made a
lot of mess. I didn't like them.'

MacDeth stopped crying. His
weeping turned into a whimper.

He rocked from side to side. 'When it all went wrong,' the rat continued, 'Alistair worked out what the problem was straightaway. He's such a brilliant man. I knew he would find a solution. He told me all about it. He said it had something to do with gaps in the DNA sequence. The DNA helix was restructuring itself. I didn't really understand. I'm not a scientist. I only looked after Mummy ... that's what I did, you see, I took care of her. And when Alistair asked me to help him, I couldn't say no. Mummy always said it was my responsibility to look after her, and I did. That's why I ended up like this, because I wanted to help Mummy.'

MacDeth sniffed and wiped his nose on his sleeve. Mum had calmed down enough to approach him again.

'Tell me,' she said to MacDeth, 'are we the first people you've kidnapped to use in your work?'

MacDeth's tear-stained face rose from the floor. 'Yes,' he croaked. 'Since the changes started, I've been too afraid to let anyone out of the castle. I had to lock them up. I couldn't take the risk that they would . . . But everything will be gone soon: food, medicines, everything!' MacDeth shuddered. 'That's why I had to send Clive and Lewis to find fresh bodies. They were the only two capable of bringing someone back. As for the others, Helen is too weak and Alfred . . . well, your children saw what happened to Alfred.' He closed his eyes and pressed his face to the floor. 'Mother ate him. They're all getting out of control. I had to do something!'

MacDeth started to cry again. Mum went to the table where MacDeth had injected himself and flicked through a pile of books and papers. Every so often, she looked up at the jars on the shelves. Finally, she clenched her fists and leant on the table with her head down.

'You can help me, can't you?' MacDeth asked. 'I mean, you are superheroes. Isn't that what superheroes do? Help people?'

Mum said nothing. Dad walked over to MacDeth and held out his hand.

'Yes, we do help people,' he said. 'And I promise we'll do everything possible to sort this out.'

93

MacDeth grabbed Dad's hand like it was a rope thrown to a drowning man.

'Oh, thank you,' he said. 'I knew you would, I just knew it. As soon as I found out you were superheroes, I knew I had a chance to change things. If anyone could show me where I had gone wrong, it was you . . . Ms Victory.' He stared at Mum and then glanced at Dad, Emma and me. 'And you're Captain Valiant, Moon Girl and

Dynamo Boy, aren't you? I only know one British superhero team, so it must be you.'

'Actually,' I said, 'my name is Dynamic Boy.'

'Is it?' MacDeth frowned. 'I'm sure if you check, you'll find it's Dynamo Boy. I'm very good with names.'

'But not much good with all the scientific stuff,' Emma muttered.

'Of course,' MacDeth said, getting up from the floor and brushing himself down, 'now that we're going to work together, I suppose we should be on first name terms. I had your cases and bags brought from the car. They're upstairs. I'm afraid the car is at the bottom of the loch. My castle is the only building for miles around and I didn't want anyone thinking you might be here – but I needed your cases and bags. I had to find out if you had any allergies or were taking any medications. I had to know as much as I could about you before I got to work . . . Louise.'

He offered Mum his hand. She ignored him. His hand turned into a fist.

'There's no need to be like that,' he said. 'Now that we'll be working together, we need to be nice to each other.' MacDeth looked up at the specimen jars. He smiled as if proud of what he saw. 'Yes, we have to be nice to each other, because if you're not nice, then you won't respect my work. And I won't allow that. No, I won't allow anyone to treat my work with disrespect. That's why you have to fix things for me. I won't have my work ridiculed. I'd rather destroy it all than have anyone laugh at what I've achieved.'

MacDeth now stood with both fists clenched,  as if ready for a fight. The determined look on his face made me think that he'd forgotten exactly what he'd achieved – the monsters he'd created and the fact that he'd been about to kill four innocent people. 'But no one will laugh

at me when my experiments are complete,' he
went on. 'Once I've succeeded, everyone will
show me the respect I deserve.' He grinned and
rocked on his feet like an overexcited child.
'Perhaps, when you've done what I want, I might
even become part of your superhero team. Yes,

you'd like that, wouldn't you? It would be good if I could work with you when everyone is well again. Mother will be so proud of me when I become part of your team.'

CHAPTER 8

It took some time for any of us to know what to say after that. I think we all thought it best to do and say nothing until we had a chance to talk alone. It wasn't until Mum got to the second suitcase and started lifting out the clothes that Emma said what was probably going through all our minds.

'I'm not an expert in this kind of thing,' she said, 'but does everyone else think MacDeth is

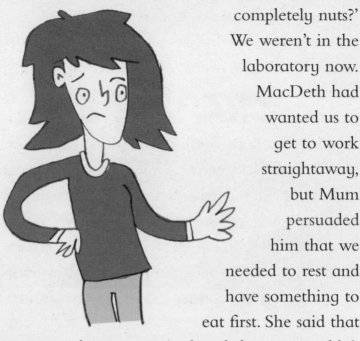

completely nuts?' We weren't in the laboratory now. MacDeth had wanted us to get to work straightaway, but Mum persuaded him that we needed to rest and have something to eat first. She said that even superheroes got tired and that we wouldn't be at our best if he rushed us.

MacDeth didn't like this at all. He stormed about the laboratory, wringing his hands and muttering under his breath. He pulled his hair, kicked tables and chairs, threw books on the floor and punched the walls. It was only when Mum said that if he carried on like this he was going to give her a terrible headache and make her feel quite ill, that he quietened down and did as she asked.

Reluctantly, he led us out of the lab, up two flights of curving stairs and along an echoing corridor until we came to an ornately carved wooden door at the end of a landing that overlooked a dark, dusty hall. Opening the door, MacDeth walked across a musty-smelling room and pulled back a pair of faded, red curtains to reveal a large four-poster bed and a dressing table cluttered with family photographs. There were holiday snaps, school photos and graduation pictures. I recognised MacDeth in some of them.

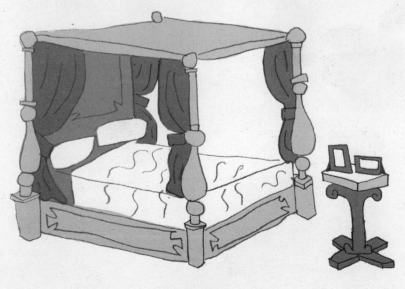

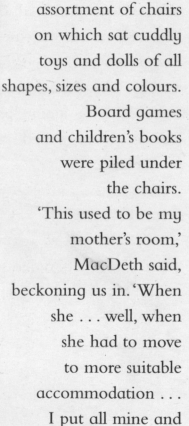

I guessed the other people were his mum, dad and sister. Lined against the walls were an assortment of chairs on which sat cuddly toys and dolls of all shapes, sizes and colours. Board games and children's books were piled under the chairs. 'This used to be my mother's room,' MacDeth said, beckoning us in. 'When she . . . well, when she had to move to more suitable accommodation . . . I put all mine and

Helen's things in here. I thought it would be better if we kept everything in one place. Mother always liked things to be tidy.'

Our suitcases were beside the bed. There were three of them and they had all been opened and the contents disturbed. Our wash bags had been emptied next to the cases. Tins of anti-perspirant, soap, shower gel, shampoo, toothpaste and toothbrushes had been arranged in neat rows. Even Dad's electric razor had been taken from its case and laid out with the electrical cord curled round it.

MacDeth stared at the bed. It was as if he was looking at something only he could see – perhaps a memory of his mother, propped up on her pillows, telling him off for not being tidy.

'I'll get you some food,' he said. 'I'm afraid it'll only be porridge and toast. You do like porridge, don't you? I've eaten porridge ever since I was a boy. Mother always said it was good for me.'

He frowned, still staring at the bed. He nodded as if someone had told him what to do.

'Oh yes,' he said, 'I almost forgot. There's a bathroom opposite if you need to freshen up. I'll bring you some clean towels.'

With a final glance at the bed, he left, closing the door behind him. As soon as he'd gone, Mum got to work on the suitcases.

'He is, isn't he?' Emma said. 'MacDeth is completely nuts.'

Mum finished her inspection of the second suitcase and started on the third. She seemed to be looking for something. Emma and I sat on the bed watching her. Dad stood by the windows, trying to open them and let some fresh air in. He'd already snapped one latch and now he was trying to open the second without breaking it. He looked over his shoulder at Mum.

'Louise,' he said, 'why don't you leave that and sit down?'

Mum said nothing. Dad turned from the window, came across and reached for her hand. She snatched it away from him.

'Please, Robert,' she said, 'I'm not in the mood

for . . .' She took a deep breath. 'I'm sorry. I didn't mean to snap. It's just . . .'

'Well, I definitely think he's nuts,' Emma said, picking up her toiletries and putting them in her wash bag. 'I mean, only a complete loony would leave the four of us in a room together. After all, we're superheroes. Doesn't he  realise we're going to think up a way to stop him doing any more experiments?'

'Don't call him nuts, Emma,' Mum said. 'MacDeth is a very sick man.'

'He's a total nutter who needs locking up,' Emma replied.

'He's mentally ill,' Mum said. 'Even though he did those awful experiments and was going to cut us up – in some respects, he's not responsible for his actions. He's not thinking rationally. That's why he's left us together. He's convinced we're going to help him.'

'Well, I say it's about time we un-convince him.' Emma threw her wash bag down. 'I mean, how could he do this to his family and friends? How could he turn them into monsters?'

Mum glanced at Dad as if expecting him to have an answer. He shook his head and went back to the window. Mum stared at the floor. She didn't seem to know what to say. 'Exactly,' Emma said. 'He's a total nutter.' Mum sighed. 'We are dealing with a man who needs psychiatric care,' she replied. 'Calling him names isn't going to help.'

Glass shattered. Dad had managed to open the window, only this time he'd broken the pane rather than the latch.

'Well, even if MacDeth is ill,' I said, 'Emma's right. We have to do something to stop him.'

'Of course we have to do something,' Mum replied. 'But we're not miracle workers, Mark. DNA isn't like a computer program that can be rebooted if it goes wrong. It's too complex. There are too many variations in its structure. Why do you think MacDeth's experiments went wrong? It's impossible to fix what he's done. His friends and family can't be changed back into the people they were and as for MacDeth, well, I'm fairly certain he's going to become just like them. I doubt if there's any way to stop the alteration in his cell structure.'

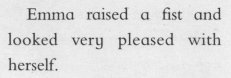

Emma raised a fist and looked very pleased with herself.

'So even if he is mentally ill,' she said, 'it makes no difference. We get to do our superhero stuff. We beat up MacDeth and his monsters and . . . well, I'm not sure about the next bit – but I'd feel a lot better if I could beat something up.'

'Yes, but the next bit is the problem, isn't it?' Mum said. 'After we've done the superhero stuff, what then? Do we hand MacDeth and his monsters over to the police? They'll probably hand them over to other scientists who will examine and study them. Because that's what will happen, Emma. Scientists don't abandon research just because the results aren't what they expected. They try again, and someone will try to create hybrid DNA again. Whether it's right or wrong doesn't matter to people who think knowledge is more important than anything else. So if we don't deal with this properly, it's very likely that the monsters you've seen in this castle will be created in laboratories across the world, and if that happens, do you really think the four of us will be able to do anything about it?'

Emma folded her arms and grunted. 'Well, I'd still feel a lot better if I could beat something up,' she said.

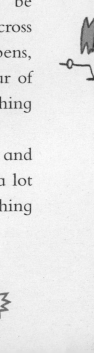

Mum was about to speak again when she was interrupted by a clatter and a scratching. I felt something brush against my legs. I had a good idea what it was. The noise had come from under the bed, and there was only one thing I could think of that was small enough to get under the bed. She must have followed us up from the lab and sneaked in while MacDeth was showing us the room, and now she had heard everything we'd said!

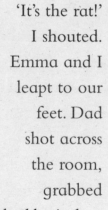

'It's the rat!' I shouted. Emma and I leapt to our feet. Dad shot across the room, grabbed the bed by its legs and lifted the whole thing off the floor. Of course, he didn't think about the height of the room or the size of the bed. The posts at the corners

smashed into the ceiling and got stuck in the rafters. Plaster fell in crumbling lumps and thudded against the carpet.

The four of us managed to get out of the way. Even Dad avoided the worst of the falling plaster.

The rat wasn't so lucky. Although she was still breathing, the rodent lay motionless on her side with a bad gash across the back of her bulbous head. In a blur of movement, Mum picked up a suitcase, put some clothes in it and laid the rat in the middle of the clothes. She then gently closed the lid and locked it.

'Robert,' she said, 'put some air holes in the top. At least this is one of MacDeth's creatures we don't have to worry about for the moment.'

Dad jabbed his finger through the case, following the edge so that he wouldn't stab the rat. It was as I watched him that I noticed a thick, white liquid seeping under the door. I knew what the liquid was. I'd seen it before, only then it had dripped down a wall.

I ran to the door. Outside, I found a tray on the floor. There were smashed plates and bowls around it. The broken pieces lay in a large puddle of steaming porridge. Slices of toast floated across the puddle.

It must have been MacDeth. I wondered how

long he had been standing outside the door, listening to us. Given the fact that he'd dropped the tray, it must have been long enough to hear that we weren't going to do what he wanted. And after the way he'd reacted when Mum had asked for some time to rest before we started work, I knew he'd be furious. He'd probably now decided that the best thing to do was go back to his original plan and use us as spare parts.

I was about to tell the others what I'd found when Dad's hand gripped my shoulder. As I turned to face him, I saw my Dynamic Boy costume in his other hand.

'Your mother hid these in the suitcases in case we might need them,' he said. 'Put it on. The holiday's over – it's time to get to work.'

CHAPTER 9

With my costume on, I suppose I should have felt a bit more like getting to work than I did. As the four of us walked out of the room, stepping over the puddle of porridge and toast, I should have felt ready to go after MacDeth in the same way as I had all the other super villains and mad scientists we'd fought before. But I didn't. Something wasn't right about this.

And I don't think I was the only one who had doubts about what we were doing. We were all very quiet as we walked along the corridor, following the trail of porridgy footprints MacDeth had left behind. Mum didn't give any orders, Dad didn't tell any bad jokes and Emma didn't grumble or complain. The only sound that followed us was our footsteps.

It was what Mum had said about Dr MacDeth being ill which bothered me. MacDeth

wasn't the usual kind of mad scientist we fought. I mean, we called them mad because they had a crazy plan to take over the world. MacDeth didn't have a crazy plan to take over the world. He'd only tried to cure his sick mother. I suppose he'd believed, if his experiments had worked, that his research would help everyone.

So it wasn't right to call Dr MacDeth mad. He

really was ill, and a man as ill as MacDeth didn't need beating up by superheroes. He needed looking after. He needed special care to help him get well . . . although he wasn't going to get well, was he? If Mum was right, MacDeth was going to become a monster just like the others. So I suppose we didn't really have a choice. We had to do the superhero thing. MacDeth wasn't going to give up his experiments. We had to fight the man and the monsters he'd created because it was the only way to sort this out.

A part of me hoped that once we had MacDeth and his monsters under control, we might be able to think of a way to help them, but I doubted it. Maybe this mess would always be a mess and we just had to clear it up as best we could.

It wasn't difficult finding the laboratory again. Despite the fact that MacDeth's porridgy footprints soon disappeared, Mum remembered the way. I nearly said something about how it would have been nice if she'd been able to remember the way back to the motorway when Dad had got lost on the back roads, but I didn't.

The laboratory was in a part of the castle where the white walls were streaked with cobwebs and mildew. The door was old and rickety with scratched, wooden panels and a

loose handle. A single lightbulb hung from the ceiling above it. I could easily imagine MacDeth and his sister as children, crouching outside the door, listening to the strange sounds coming from within.

'It's unlocked,' Dad said, turning the handle and pulling the door open.

'Of course it is,' Mum replied. 'There's no reason to lock it now. MacDeth will need more than a key to keep the four of us out.'

Three steps led down to a narrow, stone archway through which we could see the laboratory. The lights were on and nothing seemed to have changed since we'd left.

'Does anyone else think this isn't a good idea?' Emma asked.

'A few minutes ago you wanted to do some beating up,' I replied.

'Yes, well maybe I prefer to hit people who can hit back.' Emma thumped me. 'That feels better.' She went to hit me again, only Dad took her arm and pulled her into the laboratory. Mum and I

followed. As the four of us stood in the middle of the room, looking up at the specimen jars, a gust of cold air whipped around our legs.

'I can smell disinfectant,' I said.

The metal door that led into the brick corridor was open. As we walked towards it, the grey edge caught the light and shone like the blade of an axe, waiting to fall.

'You see?' Emma said. 'I told you this wasn't a good idea.'

In fact, it was a really bad idea. As we walked under the metal, we saw that every door along the corridor was open. Dad raised his hand and indicated that he wanted us to stay where we were. Slowly, he went from cell to cell and peered inside. When he got to the last one, he turned round and faced us. 'They're empty,' he said. Yes, they were empty – but that was because the things that had been inside were waiting for us in the gloom at the far end of the corridor. We didn't even have time to shout a warning to Dad.

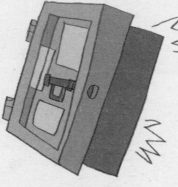

The first creature screeched and swooped down in a flurry of black feathers and slashing talons. I couldn't see the thing clearly. It moved so fast, all I could make out were wings and a beak and legs. It looked like a cross between a man and a crow. Dad disappeared under the wings as the screech turned to a squawk and a long, thin head with a pointed skull pecked at him.

This must have been the second creature that attacked the car. The one I'd seen in the car's headlights — the insect man — now flew towards Mum, Emma and me. It was just as I remembered it: thin and scrawny with wings, sharp claws and snapping mandibles. Only this

time it had no gas to knock us out. The creature had to fight us on its own – which is why we were able to beat it so easily.

Emma grabbed the insect man with her thoughts and pinned him against the roof. Mum dashed under the creature to help Dad fight the crow man, but she needn't have bothered. He'd already picked the thing up and hurled it against the wall.

The bony head cracked against the brick. The crow tried to get up. It staggered and stumbled, leapt at Dad, but only managed to crash into the wall again. For a second time, its head bounced off the brick. Then the crow fell to the floor in a heap of feathers and lay still.

The way Mum and Dad looked at the creature's body, I had the feeling the crow wasn't going to get up again.

'Well, that wasn't so bad,' Emma said. She looked up at the insect man and spun him round on the ceiling. The creature hissed and spat, speckling the walls with drool. As the drool splashed on my shoulder, I went to tell Emma to put him in one of the cells so that I could lock him in. Only I found myself staring at Dr MacDeth instead.

He was behind us in the laboratory, standing near the metal door with a large, red petrol can in his hand. I wasn't sure what he was going to do with the petrol, but I wasn't taking any chances. I grabbed Emma and pulled her out of the way.

It was a good job I did. The metal door slammed down. If I hadn't moved her, Emma would have been sliced in two. Not that she was grateful. I had to dodge punches and ignore a lot of bad language before we both realised that, now she'd lost her concentration, the insect man was free. He'd dropped from the ceiling and landed next to us. Before we could stop him, he'd grabbed both of us by the throat.

Thankfully, Dad saw what happened. He shot along the corridor like a bullet and rammed the insect man into the metal door. The creature

exploded like a fly against a windscreen. Thick, red gunge spurted over Dad, the door and the walls. The insect man's head, arms and legs flew in different directions while the rest of him stuck to the metal. His wings slid down and lay in a pool of blood and bone – a pool over which a fine mist of smoke now spread.

So that's what MacDeth had planned to do with the petrol – set fire to his laboratory! I remembered what he'd said about destroying his work rather than have anyone laugh at it. I also remembered what Mum had said about MacDeth not thinking rationally. Didn't he realise the risks? He couldn't control the fire. It would destroy everything and everyone.

Emma was right – the man was completely nuts!

'Mum!' I shouted. 'It's MacDeth, he's —'

'I know what he's doing, Mark,' Mum replied. She ran towards us from the far end of the corridor. Her costume was smoke stained and she coughed. 'I've just been to the room where you and Emma were held. It's also on fire.'

CHAPTER 10

Well, that was just brilliant. Here we were, four superheroes, trapped in a burning building and not one of us with a superpower which could fight fire or smoke! My eyes were already watering and I was finding it difficult to breathe. We gathered together at the far end of the corridor where the secret passage down from the bedroom ended and where the smoke was at its thinnest.

Looking up the brick tunnel, I saw flashes of

flame along the walls. It was easy to imagine the inferno the bedroom had become. This was an old castle with lots of old, wooden floors and old, wooden beams. It wouldn't take much to set the whole place alight. The way Emma had destroyed the bed when we'd tried to break down the door had probably made MacDeth's job a lot easier. All he had to do was gather the broken bits together and douse them in petrol. If he broke the windows as well, the fire would have plenty of oxygen and would spread very quickly, perhaps too quickly.

I looked at the wall behind me. The windows . . . if I remembered the layout of the room correctly, they were above us. That meant this was an outside wall, and if it was, then we had our way out, even though it was a very dangerous way out.

When I told Mum what I was thinking, Emma thumped me again.

'Are you mad?' she cried. 'If Dad smashes a hole in the wall, we'll end up feeding the fire more oxygen. This whole place will go up in seconds!'

'And if we don't get out of here, we'll suffocate in minutes,' Mum said. 'Robert, knock this wall down. You'll fly me and Emma out. Mark will follow us. We have to get clear of the castle as quickly as possible.'

'But what if Mark's wrong?' Emma said. 'What if there's a

corridor on the other side, or a room or something big, ugly and horrible waiting to attack us?'

'Then we'll wait here and you can go first,' Mum replied.

Dad punched the wall. Thankfully, I was right. The brick exploded outwards and cold, grey light rushed in. I could almost hear the grateful roar of

the flames – not that we gave them time to show their gratitude. With Mum and Emma in his arms, and me behind him, Dad dived through the wall and flew across the loch.

A thunderous blast quickly followed us.

It was so powerful, I almost went head over heels. As it was, I spun out of control so that, when I was finally able to look back at the castle, everything was blurred. But I couldn't miss the huge, jagged hole where we'd just stood. The walls and battlements above the hole sagged and crumbled. Slabs of brick and stone splashed into the loch as flames roared through the wall.

'We don't have much time,' Mum said. 'Nothing can stop the fire now. I hate to think how many explosive chemicals MacDeth has stored in that place. We have to go back and try to rescue whoever's still alive.'

I think Mum was the only one who thought we ought to go back. I certainly didn't want to. From what I could see, most of the castle was burning. Every window I looked at glowed bright yellow and black smoke poured from every tower. It looked like MacDeth had doused the entire building in petrol.

'Louise,' Dad said, 'if we fly in there, we may not be able to fly out again.'

'But we have to, Robert. We can't let MacDeth kill himself and his family!'

'Why don't we fly over the top?' I said. 'It'll be hot, but at least we'll be able to see into the castle. If MacDeth's there and we can reach him, Emma could lift him out with her thoughts.'

'And what if I don't want to lift him out with my thoughts?' Emma grumbled.

'Then you can watch him die,' I said. 'Would that make you happy?'

Emma didn't reply. She gave me a look, which made me feel very guilty. I was being unfair. I knew she wouldn't let MacDeth die if she could save him. But Mum was right. We had to do something other than watch the castle burn and I felt bad for not wanting to go back. I wasn't angry with Emma. I was angry with myself.

Dad considered my plan for a few moments, then gave a grim nod. We shot back to the castle, went high over the battlements and hovered above the main courtyard where the smoke wasn't as thick. The heat was much worse than I'd imagined. It felt as if my lungs burnt with every breath.

'There he is!' Mum shouted.

MacDeth limped across the courtyard below us with his head down and his hands over his face. His clothes were charred rags. It looked as if he'd got a bit too close to the flames.

He wasn't alone. Behind him, dragging itself across the stone, was another one of his creatures.

It had a long, black, glistening body like a slug —
two arms, two legs and no head. The arms and
legs pushed the body across the stone. A pair of
eyestalks twitched at the front and, all along the
body, tentacles writhed and twisted like hair
caught in the wind.

This had to be MacDeth's mother. She was the
only creature we hadn't seen properly, and those
black tentacles looked just like the thing which
had tried to grab my foot.

'Emma, get him!' Mum cried.

'I'm trying to,' Emma shouted. 'But there's something holding him down!'

That's when I saw one of the creature's tentacles wrapped around MacDeth's waist.

'It's his mother!' I shouted. 'She's holding on to him. She won't let go!'

There was another explosion. The base of the tower nearest to us ignited like the engines of a rocket. A cloud of flame and smoke rolled up the stone. This time, the force of the blast knocked us out of the sky as if we'd been swatted by a giant hand.

Dad managed to keep hold of Mum and Emma, but went whirling down into the courtyard. I was blown into the highest window of the tower opposite. I was lucky I didn't go through the glass. Instead, the panes cracked and my costume became snagged on the jagged edges.

Mum, Dad and Emma weren't so lucky. They had fallen on to the slug. All three of them were now trapped in its black tentacles. Emma's head and neck were completely covered. Mum was wrapped from her feet to her throat. Dad had ripped and torn every tentacle that wound itself around him, but for every tentacle he destroyed, two more took its place. He was fighting a losing battle.

Which left only me, and I had no idea what to do. I knew I had to get free, so I turned and smashed the window with my feet, kicking out the panes. Glancing into the room behind the

glass, I saw a suitcase on the floor and a four-poster bed hanging from the ceiling.

It was our suitcase, the one with the rat inside! I'd been blown across the courtyard into the window of the room where MacDeth had taken us after we'd left the laboratory – his mother's room. It wasn't full of smoke and I could see everything clearly: the chairs with toys on them and the family photographs on the dressing table.

The family photographs! Now I had an idea what to do. I smashed my way into the room, grabbed the suitcase, snatched a photograph from the dressing table and flew out, shooting down into the courtyard.

I landed in front of MacDeth and his mother. The slug's eyestalks jerked to stare at me and a tentacle snaked out. I put the suitcase down and threw open the lid. The rat was conscious now. She must have been waiting for a chance to escape. She leapt out and fell to the ground, scrabbling at the stone to get away from me. Her bloody, deformed head got in the way of her flailing claws.

I picked the rat up by the scruff of the neck and showed her the photograph.

'Is this your mother?' I yelled. 'Is this your mother?'

The rat didn't reply. She squealed and hissed. Before I could get an answer, a black tentacle went round the rat's body and wrenched it from my grasp.

'Mummy,' the rat shrieked, 'they hurt me! They hit me on the head and locked me in the dark!'

Hearing his sister's voice, MacDeth took his hands from his face. I wished he

hadn't. He had been horribly burnt. Half his face had been turned into a smouldering mess of blackened flesh. MacDeth must have set himself alight when he'd started the fires. He pointed at me and shouted, 'They wouldn't help me, Mother. This is all their fault. I didn't want this to happen. They did it! If they'd helped me none of this would have happened!'

So much for trying to save MacDeth and his family. I now only had one chance to save my own family and I wasn't going to waste it. I looked at the photograph. It was a picture of a woman and two children at the seaside. It must have been MacDeth, his sister and mother. Perhaps if they saw themselves at a happier time it might be enough to make them forget the horror of their present – and about Dad, Mum, Emma and me for a few seconds. I had to create an illusion they would be desperate to believe.

I made the woman and children in the photograph appear next to me, just as they were in the picture, with the same clothes and the same

smiles. I made the woman wrap her arms around the children, kiss their faces and hug them.

And it worked! The slug stopped moving and its tentacles went limp. The rat and MacDeth fell silent and stared at the illusion. I saw Dad tear himself free of the slug's grip and speed across to Mum and Emma. Glancing in my direction, he ripped apart the tentacles and then shot up into the sky with Mum and Emma in his arms.

I was quick to follow. As I took off, I heard MacDeth say, 'You see, Mother, you're better now. I told you I could do it. I told you!' And then they were gone. We left them behind in the flames: MacDeth, his sister and his mother.

Once again, the four of us were speeding across the loch and, this time, there was no going back. We only stopped when a third explosion thundered across the water, and the sky around us glowed a deep red.

There was no hope of anyone surviving this third blast. The castle collapsed. The last two towers fell and the walls caved in. The courtyard where we had left MacDeth, his mother and his sister, disappeared under burning bricks. Fire blazed across the loch and smoke rolled over the water. It seemed MacDeth had finally succeeded in doing something he really wanted – he had destroyed his family, his friends and all his work. He'd made sure no one would ever laugh at him or what he'd achieved.

I don't know how long we watched the castle

burn. We'd tried to do what was right, but we couldn't save MacDeth and his family. Sometimes, even when you're a superhero, you have to fight battles you can't win. The best you can hope for is that you walk away from them in one piece.

A cold wind blew against my back. It went through the holes in my costume left by the

broken window. As the cuts and grazes on my back smarted, I felt rain on my face.

'We need to go,' Mum said. 'There's no more we can do here. The fire will burn itself out. When we get back home, I'll make sure someone knows what's happened. Maybe we'll come back and help clear up the . . .' Her voice cracked. I didn't need to look at her to know there were tears in her eyes.

We all watched the castle burn as the wind got stronger and the rain got heavier. It was only when all our faces were wet enough to hide our tears, that Dad turned away and stared out at the horizon. It seemed as if he had something important to say.

'I don't suppose any of you know the way back to England?' he said. 'I don't want to get lost again.'

HAVE YOU READ...

REVENGE OF THE BLACK PHANTOM

Mark Taylor seems to be an average schoolboy, but he's really Dynamic Boy!

He and his family – Captain Valiant, Ms Victory and Moon Girl – are a superhero team. If only his name, costume and superpower weren't so rubbish, Dynamic Boy might enjoy saving the world from baddies . . .

But when people start turning into monsters, they all realise this is no ordinary baddy – it's the revenge of the Black Phantom.

RETURN
OF THE
SILVER CYBORG

Mark Taylor, aka Dynamic Boy, and his superhero family are under threat from an evil techno-genius. The Silver Cyborg's got a devious new plan – he's going to trap them in the world of Dynamic Boy's mind! How will their superpowers save them from the dangers of Mark's imagination? And will Mark ever survive the embarrassment of his family seeing his deepest, secret wishes? It could be his biggest challenge ever!

THE MAN WHO STOLE A PLANET

Dynamic Boy and his superhero family are caught up in a space battle between the Federal Army of the Republic of Taranos (FART) and the Bureau of Undercover Research Personnel (BURP).

A BURP agent has stolen a secret weapon from the FART – the Eternity Stone, which can shrink planets to the size of a matchbox. It's up to our heroes to recapture the device before BURP and FART tear the galaxy apart!

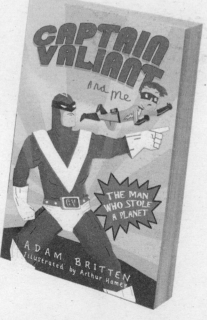

piccadillypress.co.uk/children

Go online to discover:

☆ more authors you'll love

☆ competitions

☆ sneak peeks inside books

☆ fun activities and downloads